Welcome to the Forest, where
THE MINISTRY OF MONSTERS
helps humans and monsters live side
by side in peace and harmony...

CONNOR O'GOYLE
lives here too, with his gargoyle mum,
human dad and his dog, Trixie.
But Connor's no ordinary boy...

When monsters get out of control,
Connor's the one for the job.
He's half-monster, he's the Ministry's
NUMBER ONE AGENT,
and he's licensed to do things
no one else can do. He's...

MONSTER BOY!

First published in 2009 by Orchard Books
First paperback publication in 2010

ORCHARD BOOKS
338 Euston Road, London NW1 3BH
Orchard Books Australia
Level 17/207 Kent St, Sydney, NSW 2000

ISBN 978 1 40830 246 0 (hardback)
ISBN 978 1 40830 254 5 (paperback)

Text and illustrations © Shoo Rayner 2009

1 3 5 7 9 10 8 6 4 2 (hardback)
1 3 5 7 9 10 8 6 4 2 (paperback)

Printed in Great Britain

Orchard Books is a division of Hachette Children's Books,
an Hachette UK company.

www.hachette.co.uk

SIREN SPELL

SHOO RAYNER

ORCHARD BOOKS

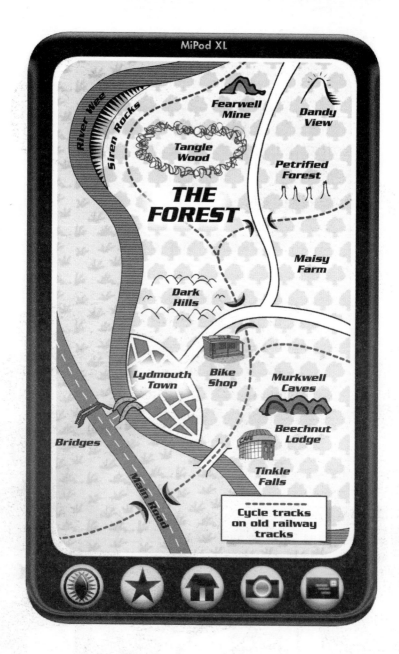

"Are you coming to watch me race?"
Dad asked Connor at breakfast.
Dad was home to compete in
the Forest Mountain Bike
Championship.

"Of course!" Connor grinned. "Trixie and I will be cheering you all the way."

"I'm afraid I'm busy," Connor's mum said. "*Monsters of Pop* are holding auditions in the Forest today."

"*Monsters of Pop*? Do you mean the TV talent show?" asked Dad. "What's that got to do with you?"

Mum smiled sweetly. "I'm going to enter. I love the judge, Simon Bull. He's so dreamy!"

Monsters of POP

on Bull

There was a moment of silence before Connor and his dad exploded into fits of giggling. "But you ca-ha-ha-n't sing!" they chorused.

"I can too!" Mum snapped. She opened her mouth wide. A deafening wail, like a sick cat, filled the room. Connor and Dad covered their ears.

Trixie joined in, howling at the top of her voice. She loved Mum's singing.

"If you pass your audition," Dad laughed, "I'll eat my cycle shorts!"

In the middle of all the racket, Connor's MiPod beeped.

MISSION ALERT!

To: Monster Boy,
Number One Agent

From: Mission Control,
Ministry of Monsters

Subject: It's the Forest Mountain
Bike Championship today

We need you on patrol to attend to any emergencies. Some monsters might get a little overexcited.

Please leave immediately.

Good luck!

M.O.M.

THIS MESSAGE WILL SELF-ERASE IN FIFTEEN SECONDS

"Sorry, Dad," said Connor. "The Ministry of Monsters needs me today. I might not be able to see all of your race."

Dad looked disappointed. "Oh, that's all right, son. I understand."

Connor's mum looked after his amazing
Monster Bikes at the Pedal-O bike shop
where they lived. A few minutes later
she had Connor's high-tech bike,
MB6, ready for a hard day on patrol.

"I've made you lots of sandwiches and there's a big bottle of water," Mum told Connor. "Do be careful."

"Oh, *Mum!*" Connor sighed. "I'll be fine."

Connor's mum was a Gargoyle, so Connor was half-monster. His code-name was Monster Boy. If anyone could look after himself, Connor could.

As he set off down the cycle path, Connor called back to his mum, "I'm more worried about you, actually. Please don't go to the *Monsters of Pop* audition. You'll only embarrass yourself!"

"Werr-ruff!" Trixie did not agree.

The Forest was all decked out for the Championship. Flags and banners marked the route of the race. Connor parked on top of Dandy View Hill, where he could see over the whole of the Forest.

Dad's race was late. Connor and Trixie shared the sandwiches while they waited.

They waited – and waited – and waited. Had the race been held up? Had the route of the race been changed? Had all the cyclists been swallowed up into the mysterious Dark Hills?

Connor checked the route of the race on his MiPod.

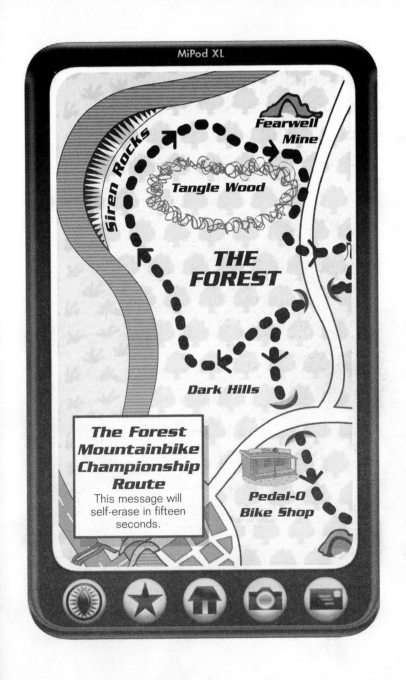

"The bikers should be here by now," Connor told Trixie. "I hope they haven't taken a wrong turn."

He studied the map for clues. "Oh no!" he gasped. "The track runs very close to the Siren Rocks. If the Sirens are out today, they could spoil everything."

Connor switched on the Directional Sound Amplifier and aimed his handlebars towards the Siren Rocks. The speakers began to play a strange, wailing music.

"Siren songs!" he wailed. "I hope we're not too late!"

MiPOD MONSTER IDENTIFIER PROGRAM

Monster:

Siren

Distinguishing Features:
Sirens are loud, raucous women with bird-like features.

Preferred Habitat:
Wild, exposed places.

Essential Information:
Sirens believe the awful sound they make is beautiful music. The noise can hypnotise a man and lure him to his doom!

Danger Rating: 4

Connor turned the amplifier off. He didn't want to be mesmerised. Searching through his equipment, he soon found his clip-on ear-defenders.

"Can you hear me?" Connor asked Trixie at the top of his voice.

"Wuff!" Trixie barked.

"What?" Connor couldn't hear a thing.

Connor zoomed up the hill in the direction of the Siren Rocks – tall cliffs that rose high on the edge of the Forest.

The three Sirens stood on the edge of the cliff. They played their harps and warbled their strange bird-like songs, luring the mountain bikers towards them.

The bikers were all hypnotised. The song had lured them away from the race track. Now, they wobbled slowly towards the edge of the cliff like a pack of zombies.

"Dad!" Connor yelled.

His dad couldn't
hear him. None
of the bikers
could. They were
entranced by the
Sirens' song.

Connor racked his brains. What could he do? Dad and the other bikers were seconds away from falling to certain doom! Connor had to distract the Sirens somehow. He had to do something – *fast!*

Connor plugged his MiPod into MB6's sound system and chose the first song that came up on the MP3 program.

Seconds later the sound of an orchestra boomed out of his bike's speakers and a crackly, old-fashioned voice began to sing: *"If you go down to the woods today, you're sure of a big surprise..."*

"Oh, *what*?" Connor couldn't believe it. "*The Teddy Bears' Picnic*? How did that get on my MiPod? It's so-o-o uncool!"

But it did the trick. The Sirens' song stopped. They couldn't keep up their rhythm while *The Teddy Bears' Picnic* drowned them out.

The cyclists shook their heads and rubbed their eyes. They couldn't remember how they had got there.

Connor's dad stopped right on the edge of the cliff and blinked.

"Dad!" Connor called. "This way! Follow the path until it brings you out on the race track again."

It took a moment for Dad to realise where he was. He leapt back on his bike and powered off down the path. "Thanks, son. See you later!" The race was back on.

When Connor was sure all the bikers were on the right track he went back to the Sirens, who stared at their birdy feet.

"Sorreee!" they said with one voice. "We just love to sing!"

Connor's MiPod beeped at that very moment. It was a text from Dad. He always sent messages at the most unhelpful times!

Connor laughed. His dad had just given him an idea. "Come with me," he told the Sirens. "I've got a job for you."

Connor arrived at the
Monsters of Pop audition just
as Mum was about to sing.

"I've got you some backing singers,"
he told her. "Trust me – I think they
might help."

Connor flipped his ear defenders down again.

Mum began singing her awful, drowned-cat song, while the Sirens booped and shoobee-dooped in the background.

The judges were mesmerised by the Sirens. They didn't notice how bad Mum's singing was.

Simon Bull, the judge with the dazzling white teeth, was transfixed. "That was the best we've heard today!" he cried. "I'm putting you through to the next round!"

Mum ran up to the judges' desk and kissed him!

When Dad came home later, he was clutching a gleaming trophy. "You're looking at the new Forest Mountain Bike Champion!" he said smugly.

"That's nice, dear," said Mum, putting his supper on the table. "You're not the only winner, you know."

The plate was filled with a pair of bright-blue Lycra cycle shorts, sitting on a pile of nice, healthy lettuce! Mum returned to the kitchen and began singing. She sounded like a parrot in a hot shower.

Trixie threw back her head and joined in joyfully. "Yow-how-yow-ow-ow-owl!"

Dad stared at Connor.
"Does this mean that Mum
passed her audition?" he
shouted over the din.

Connor was eating his supper with a peaceful smile on his face. He was wearing his bike helmet. The ear defenders were still attached.

"What?" he shouted.

SHOO RAYNER
MONSTER BOY

All priced at £3.99

The Monster Boy stories are available from all good bookshops,
or can be ordered direct from the publisher:
Orchard Books, PO BOX 29, Douglas IM99 1BQ
Credit card orders please telephone 01624 836000
or fax 01624 837033 or visit our website: www.orchardbooks.co.uk
or e-mail: bookshop@enterprise.net for details.

To order please quote title, author and ISBN
and your full name and address.
Cheques and postal orders should be made payable to 'Bookpost plc.'
Postage and packing is FREE within the UK
(overseas customers should add £2.00 per book).

Prices and availability are subject to change.